D1171713

The Seventh Mirror

The Seventh Mirror

TERRY KAY

MERCER UNIVERSITY PRESS
MACON, GEORGIA

MUP/ H874

1400 Coleman Avenue
Macon, Georgia 31207

First Edition

Books published by Mercer University Press are printed on acid-free paper that meets the requirements of the American National Standard for Information Sciences—Permanence of Paper for Printed Library Materials.

Mercer University Press is a member of Green Press Initiative (greenpressinitiative.org), a nonprofit organization working to help publishers and printers increase their use of recycled paper and decrease their use of fiber derived from endangered forests. This book is printed on recycled paper.

ISBN 978-0-88146-452-8

Cataloging-in-Publication Data is available from the Library of Congress

One night I dreamed about the story that is told in this book. It was not a new experience. I dream when I sleep—brief naps or for long hours—but I seldom remember what the dream was about. This story was different, perhaps because I thought it would be a good tale for my grandchildren. Point is, I did remember it and I then did what all writers tend to do: I began asking that joyful "what if...?" question that teases the imagination. The words fall off the fingers faster and better when that teasing takes place. It makes me eager to discover where the words are leading me. If there is a better reason for writing, I am not aware of it.

Because I believed my grandchildren and great-grandchildren would find pleasure in a story made from a dream, this book is dedicated to them and to all children in all places. I hope they find their own Seventh Mirror and become what they wish to be.

And there is another person who has been such a believer in this story that it belongs to him almost as much as it belongs to me. His name is Jack Osteen, a long-time and cherished friend. For many years Jack has read this story to students at a school in Columbus, Georgia, and each year he has sent me expressions of their exuberance. I know this about Jack: he is exactly what he should have been—a good and caring man.

—Terry Kay

VII
T.K.

His name was Fergus Greybar the Fourth, although everyone called him the Mirror Man because he lived in a wagon of mirrors pulled by two magnificent white horses named Look and See.

To everyone who saw it rolling slowly along the narrow roads of the countryside, the wagon looked exactly like a small house.

It was covered with boards that had been painted a gleaming white.

It had a bright red roof and bright red window shutters at tiny windows that were on both sides of the wagon.

Small flower boxes were beneath the windows, filled with yellow-eyed daisies and little sprigs of herbs that the Mirror Man used for cooking.

A red door was at the back of the wagon, with red steps that could unfold to touch the ground.

Underneath the wagon were four pull-out drawers. One contained cooking utensils. One was a table. One stored the Mirror Man's clothes. The fourth was a bed, where the Mirror Man slept when the weather was cool and pleasant and the night sky was filled with star-winks.

On the sides of the wagon, these words had been painted:

COME AND SEE YOURSELF AS ONLY YOU CAN
LOOK IN THE MIRRORS OF THE MIRROR MAN

Everywhere the Mirror Man went, grown-ups gathered with their children to marvel at his wagon house and to pay their pennies to look into the mirrors inside it.

"How can this be?" the grown-ups muttered with amazement. "Outside, it is so small, but inside, it is as large as a great house belonging to a great man—a king, perhaps, or at least the mayor of a town."

The Mirror Man smiled when asked how his wagon-home could be so different, inside and outside.

"Magic," he answered with a wink.

And the grown-ups laughed. They no longer believed in magic. Magic was an ancient superstition, something that lived only in the imaginations of children, or in the rambling stories of the very old, who, themselves, were often like children.

***

There were seven mirrors in the Mirror Man's wagon.

Six of the mirrors made everyone look foolish and funny.

Tall and short, skinny and wide, top to bottom, side to side.

Dangling arms and stubby legs, eyes as big as ostrich eggs.

Ears that could have been anything—flying kites or turkey wings.

Feet that reached across the floor, stretching out from door to door.

Squeals of laughter always came from the Mirror Man's wagon when children looked at themselves in the six trick mirrors.

***

But it was the Seventh Mirror that was truly special.

The Seventh Mirror was at the front of the wagon, in a small, brilliantly white room that had a thick cluster of gold and yellow stars painted across the ceiling and spilling like stardust onto the walls.

On the door of the room of the Seventh Mirror, a warning had been posted:

FOR CHILDREN ONLY

"But, why?" asked the grown-ups when they came to the door. "What is in the room of the Seventh Mirror?"

And, again, the Mirror Man answered with a smile, "Magic."

And, again, the grown-ups laughed.

"The only magic here," they said, "is watching our pennies disappear into the money pouch of the Mirror Man."

But the Mirror Man knew they were wrong.

There *was* magic in the Seventh Mirror, although it looked the same as any mirror in any home or shop—toe-to-head tall and shoulder-to-shoulder wide, large enough for a person to see all of himself, or herself.

And before each child entered the room, the Mirror Man would lean to them and whisper the words taught to him by his father:

"Look into this mirror and you will see,

"Not who you are, but who you wish to be."

And that was why the Seventh Mirror was different—because it permitted children to see themselves as they dreamed of being.

Not as children, but as grown-ups.

Young girls who wanted to be ballerinas saw themselves as young ladies, dressed as dancers, in colorful, flowing skirts and ballet slippers.

Young boys who wanted to be firemen saw themselves as young men, dressed in a fireman's uniform, with a fireman's red hat and black boots.

The Seventh Mirror knew every secret dream, every true wish, of anyone who looked into it.

All kinds of dreams.

Or wishes.

For a wish is only a dream never forgotten.

And so it was that everywhere the Mirror Man went, children eagerly gathered to pet his two white horses, Look and See, and to gaze at themselves in his mirrors.

And always, after looking into the Seventh Mirror, the children would ask him, "How did it happen? How did I see myself as I wish to be when I become a grown-up?"

And the Mirror Man would smile and again he would whisper, "Magic." Then he would say, "But you must never tell the grown-ups what you have seen."

"Why?" the children would ask.

"Because grown-ups are afraid of magic," the Mirror Man would answer.

Often, the Mirror Man would think about the answer he gave to the children when telling of the Seventh Mirror, and he would feel ashamed. He knew the mirror had magic, yet he had never looked into it. Never. Not even as a young boy.

His father, Fergus Greybar the Third, had said to him, "You must see yourself in the Seventh Mirror. One day you will be the Mirror Man and you must know about it."

"I will look," he had promised his father. "Someday. Not now. Someday."

And the years had passed, and he had become the Mirror Man after his father, but he had never looked into the Seventh Mirror because he was not certain he wanted to be a Mirror Man.

What if he had become a Mirror Man only because his father and his grandfather had been Mirror Men before him?

He had known many people who became what other people expected them to be, not because it was their own dream, on their own wish.

What if he looked into the mirror and saw himself dressed as a police officer?

Or a railroad engineer, guiding large trains across the country?

Or a chef in a busy restaurant?

Or a soldier marching in a parade?

Or a fisherman casting a net over water?

There were many things he might have become, too many to count.

Sometimes, at night, when sitting in his chair beside his wagon, he would gaze at the deep purple sky above him and wonder if there was anything at all special about being a Mirror Man.

It was not easy work, as many people believed.

Sometimes jeering boys jumped out from hiding along the roadways, trying to frighten him.

Sometimes the men of the towns and villages made fun of him, saying such things as, "Why don't you join a circus, Mirror Man? You're nothing but a sideshow, and that's where sideshows should be—in a circus."

Sometimes the rain and the wind swept so furiously around his wagon-home, he was afraid it would topple over, breaking all the mirrors, or the snow would be so deep his wagon would look like an igloo.

Sometimes the sun fell over him with such blistering heat, he wondered if he would melt.

Sometimes he became so lonely he would talk for hours to Look and See, and sometimes he believed Look and See answered him.

Being a Mirror Man had hardships that other people did not understand.

Yet, there were times when he believed the most wonderful thing in the world was being exactly who he was.

Who else heard so much laughter from children?

Who else saw so many glad smiles on the faces of mothers?

Who else traveled so slowly from place to place? So slowly he could listen to concerts by birds, or watch blossoms open in distant fields, or spy on animals playing in meadows.

Who else saw wondrous displays in the heavens at night? Showers of shooting stars, the feathered tails of streaking comets, the billowing smile of the man in the moon. On those nights, Fergus Greybar the Fourth did not believe anything on Earth was better than being a Mirror Man.

It was on such a night of wonder that the Mirror Man heard a faint whimper coming from the trees near his campsite. The whimper caused Look and See to turn their heads toward the sound. The small bells on their bridles jingled. One of them whinnied softly.

"So, you heard it also," the Mirror Man said in a whisper.

The whimper from the trees grew louder.

"Who's there?" called the Mirror Man.

The whimpering stopped, and the Mirror Man heard something—or someone—moving among the trees.

A stray cat, he thought. Cats made strange, mewing sounds like whimpering.

Or perhaps it was a puppy that someone had abandoned, a puppy too small to know about the woods at night.

Or perhaps it was a group of town boys slipping into his campsite to frighten him. He knew he was not far from the village of Whistletown, where a great whistle on the top of the courthouse sounded each day at noon and again at five o'clock, signaling people to stop their work and enjoy the fellowship of their friends. Whistletown was one of his favorite places. The people who lived in Whistletown were kind and always welcomed his visits.

Still, boys were boys, and it seemed to the Mirror Man that all boys were alike in one way, regardless of where they lived: all boys played pranks.

The Mirror Man stood at his chair and peered into the dark shadows of the trees. "Who's there?" he called a second time.

He could hear soft crying, like that of a child.

"Please don't hurt me," a voice begged.

"Hurt you?" said the Mirror Man. "Why would I hurt you? I would never do that. Come forward. Let me see you."

A small girl stepped cautiously from the shadows.

Look and See bobbed their heads, the bells on their bridles jingling merrily. The girl looked at them, startled.

"Oh, don't mind Look and See," the Mirror Man said, laughing warmly. "They're not going to hurt you. They're glad to see you, that's all. They always ring their bells when they're glad to see someone. Now, come, let me have a look at you."

The girl walked slowly toward the wagon, into the light of the lantern the Mirror Man had placed on his pull-out table.

She wore a dress covered with the print of small, bright red flowers. Her hair was a soft blond-yellow in the lantern light, and though her eyes were puffed from crying, the Mirror Man could see she was very pretty. He thought she was nine or ten years old, but he was not sure. Guessing the age of someone was not easy for him. A small brown suitcase was clutched in her hands.

"Well, now," the Mirror Man said pleasantly. "I don't get many visitors who look so lovely and so sad at the same time." He bowed graciously. "My name is Fergus Greybar the Fourth, but most people call me the Mirror Man. And who would you be?"

"My name is Sarah," the girl said timidly.

"Sarah? It's a fine name, a beautiful name," the Mirror Man said.

Sarah looked warily at the strange wagon-home of the Mirror Man, with the sign that read:

COME AND SEE YOURSELF AS ONLY YOU CAN
LOOK IN THE MIRRORS OF THE MIRROR MAN

The Mirror Man laughed. "Have you ever seen yourself six feet tall?" he asked.

Sarah shook her head.

"Or wide, like this?" the Mirror Man said, spreading his arms.

Sarah again shook her head.

"Well, Sarah, if you looked into my mirrors, that's what you'd see," the Mirror Man told her. "And we'll do that later, but, first, tell me all about yourself. Do you live nearby?"

Sarah lowered her head. "In Whistletown," she said in a whisper.

"Whistletown?" said the Mirror Man. "That's not so far away, but, then, it's not so nearby, either. Were you out playing and forgot your way home?"

Sarah shook her head. "I ran away," she said.

"And why would you do that?" the Mirror Man asked gently.

"Because my parents are going to move far off, to another city, and I don't want to leave all my friends," Sarah answered.

"But haven't you already left them by running away?" the Mirror Man said.

"I'm not running away forever," Sarah replied. "When my parents have moved, I'll go back to Whistletown."

The Mirror Man nodded. "I understand," he said. "It's very hard to leave friends. But you must be hungry. I've just finished my evening meal. Have you eaten?"

Sarah looked longingly at the food still on the Mirror Man's table. "No," she answered.

"Then permit me to prepare a plate for you," the Mirror Man told her. "It's not a king's feast, but I have good bread and cheese and fish caught from a clear stream, and some grapes a farmer gave to me earlier today."

"Thank you," Sarah said. She sat wearily in the Mirror Man's chair and watched as he quickly prepared her plate.

"Don't you think your parents are worried about you?" the Mirror Man asked as he placed the food before Sarah.

"They didn't listen to me," Sarah said in a trembling voice. "They're just doing what they want to do."

The Mirror Man stroked his beard thoughtfully. "Perhaps they're doing what they believe is best for you, and for them. I'm sure they miss you, but tonight you will be my guest. Tomorrow morning, we'll think of something to do. People always think better after they've rested."

***

And, so, Sarah slept through the night in the Mirror Man's pull-out bed, while the Mirror Man paced back and forth in his camp, keeping watch over her, wondering what he would do when the morning light came up out of the darkness.

He knew he must return Sarah to her family, yet if he told her that was his plan, she might run away from him also and become too lost to be found.

"What should I do?" he whispered to Look and See.

Look and See bobbed their heads, and the tinkling of their bells rang softly over the camp.

"If only she knew what it means to have a home, no matter where that home is," the Mirror Man said.

Again Look and See bobbed their heads and, again, their bells rang softly.

The Mirror Man gazed at the sky. In the distance, he saw a brilliant silver light streak across the dark silk of night, like an arrow speeding from a bow of stars, disappearing into the cup of the Big Dipper. And the stars seemed to spin and dance gladly in the fading path of the light.

Nothing could be more magical than the night sky, he thought. Not even the Seventh Mirror.

And then an idea flashed in his mind. Of course! The Seventh Mirror. The answer to his concern for Sarah was in the Seventh Mirror. There was magic about it he had never shared with anyone. Magic that only very special people could use, because it was so powerful.

Suddenly, the Mirror Man knew what he would do.

"Yes," he said quietly.

IV

At daybreak, Sarah awoke to the scent of cooking oatmeal and bread. She sat up in the pull-out bed and saw the Mirror Man placing plates and bowls on the pullout table.

"Ah, good morning," the Mirror Man called brightly.

"Good morning," said Sarah.

"You're awake just in time," the Mirror Man told her. "I hope you like oatmeal and fresh-baked bread with some very special strawberry jam."

The thought of bread and strawberry jam made Sarah smile. "Oh, yes, very much," she said.

"Then, come, eat," urged the Mirror Man. "After breakfast, we'll brush Look and See, and then I have a treat for you."

"A treat?" said Sarah.

"You'll see," the Mirror Man replied gleefully. "You'll see."

***

After she had eaten her breakfast of oatmeal and bread and jam, and after she had helped brush Look and See until their white coats were shining in the morning sun, the Mirror Man said to Sarah, "Now, sit and wait. I'll be right back," and he disappeared into the wagon of mirrors.

Sarah sat in the chair and waited. She thought about her mother and father, and about her grandmothers and grandfathers, and about her friends, and she became sad. She knew they all were searching for her. Still, she did not want to leave Whistletown. It had always been her home. She did not want to move far away to some strange city.

***

Suddenly, the door to the wagon opened and the Mirror Man stood on the steps. He was dressed in a black tuxedo and he was wearing a tall, shiny top hat and was carrying a black walking cane with a silver knob. Sarah laughed when she saw him.

He began a wobbling little dance down the steps of the wagon.

"Miss Sarah," he said, bowing comically and extending his hand to her, "The mirrors await you."

Sarah took his hand and stood and curtsied politely, and the Mirror Man turned and led her up the steps and into the wagon.

Inside the wagon, Sarah gasped in surprise. Like everyone, she was astonished at the size of the Mirror Man's wagon-home. It was as large as a grand ballroom, or so it seemed. The ceiling was tall and had been painted a soft blue to look like the sky. In a far front corner, the yellow rays of a painted sun peeked from behind the shining white of a billowing cloud. Curtains the color of rich gold were attached to long brass rods lining both sides of the wagon, making a wide corridor that led to a door in the distance.

"How can it be so big?" asked Sarah in whispered amazement.

The Mirror Man smiled and touched his cane to the tip of his tall, silk hat. "Magic," he said. He reached for the long, braided cords attached to the curtains and pulled them slowly while making the kind of silly, funny face a clown would make, causing Sarah to giggle happily. When the curtains were completely pulled along their brass rods, Sarah could see six large mirrors – three on each side of the wagon.

Again, the Mirror Man bowed. He did a shuffling dance step and mugged a smile into the first mirror, and then he began to sing:

"Mirror, mirror on the wall,

"Am I short, or am I tall?

"Who is that, that Who I see?

"Is it it, or is it me?"

He took Sarah's hand and turned her to the mirror. Sarah squealed in delight as she saw herself no taller than a doll. The Mirror Man tugged her a step closer to the mirror and she was suddenly as tall as the Mirror Man. Sarah again squealed and clapped her hands.

The Mirror Man did another dance step around Sarah and guided her to the second mirror. He sang:

"Funny faces from here and there,

"Oh my goodness! I declare!

"Who is that, that Who I see?

"Is it it, or is it me?"

Sarah looked into the mirror. She could see her eyes looking out from the blond curls of her hair, and she reached to touch her face. Her hands disappeared into her hair. The Mirror Man knelt and placed his face beside her face, and his eyes disappeared into his hat. Sarah's laughter filled the wagon.

The Mirror Man put his hands on her shoulders and moved her to the third mirror. He sang:

"Thin or wide, or wide or thin?

"Where's my ear and where's my chin?

"Who is that, that Who I see?

"Is it it, or is it me?"

In the mirror, Sarah's body became a wide, thin line, like a pancake, and her chin disappeared. The

Mirror Man did a spinning dance step around her and sang:

"A little dot for my nose.

"Arms that go from neck to toes,

"Who is that, that Who I see?

"Is it it or is it me?"

He took Sarah by the hands and began to turn her around and around in his funny dance. Both of them sang:

"Who is that, that Who I see?

"Is it it, or is it me?"

And so they went from mirror to mirror, the Mirror Man guiding Sarah, singing his merry song. Sarah laughed and danced, twirling before the mirrors, captivated by the strange, changing images that quivered in the reflections like waves of light.

"What do you think, Miss Sarah?" asked the Mirror Man.

"I think it's wonderful," answered Sarah.

"Yes," said the Mirror Man. "But there's one more mirror."

Sarah looked at him quizzically.

"Close your eyes," the Mirror Man told her.

Sarah closed her eyes, and the Mirror Man took the curtains and pulled them back over the brass curtain rods, covering the mirrors.

"Now, give me your hand," the Mirror Man said.

Sarah offered her hand, and the Mirror Man took it and guided her down the corridor to the door at the front of the wagon.

"You may open your eyes now," the Mirror Man told her.

Sarah opened her eyes and looked up and saw the sign that read:

FOR CHILDREN ONLY

"Behind this door is another mirror," the Mirror Man said. "The Seventh Mirror. It's very special."

"Why?" asked Sarah.

The Mirror Man leaned very close to Sarah. He whispered, "Because it's the most magic of all things that are magic anywhere in the world."

"What do you mean?" said Sarah.

The Mirror Man nodded a deep, bobbing, serious nod. He put his finger to his lips in a hushing motion. And then he said:

"Look into this mirror and you will see,

"Not who you are, but who you wish to be."

Sarah smiled. The Mirror Man was a funny person. Not at all like other grown-ups she knew.

"Oh, but it's true," said the Mirror Man. "Open the door. Go inside. You'll see."

"Aren't you going with me?" asked Sarah.

"Oh, no," the Mirror Man said hastily. "No, no, no. You must go in alone." He took a step backward.

"I'll wait outside for you." He began his funny wobbling dance down the corridor of the wagon. Then he winked at Sarah and opened the door leading from the wagon and he stepped outside.

***

Sarah turned to the door of the Seventh Mirror. The Mirror Man's voice was like an echo:

"Look into this mirror and you will see,

"Not who you are, but who you wish to be."

She opened the door and stepped inside the room, and it seemed she had stepped into a cloud floating among gold and yellow stars. The mirror was against the wall. It did not look like a mirror of magic. It looked like the mirror in her mother's bedroom, only taller.

Sarah moved cautiously to stand in front of the mirror. At first, she saw only the image of herself. And then her image began to fade, until it became a shimmering white light, and out of the light, Sarah saw another image slowly appear. It was of a young woman with blond hair and a slender, pretty face. She was wearing the white uniform of a nurse.

Sarah stood staring at the mirror in awe. She could hear the whisper of the Mirror Man: " ... *not who you are, but who you wish to be."*

She had always wanted to be a nurse.

And she knew that she was looking at herself, at the vision of a wish.

Outside the wagon, the Mirror Man prepared to leave his campsite. He cleaned and put away the cooking and eating utensils, and poured water over his cook fire. He was buckling the harnesses on Look and See when the door to the wagon opened and Sarah stepped outside and stood on the top step, an expression of amazement on her face.

"You saw?" said the Mirror Man.

"Yes," answered Sarah in a soft voice.

"Ah, and what did you see?" asked the Mirror Man.

"Me. I saw me," Sarah told him. "I was a—nurse."

"But a grown-up, yes?" said the Mirror Man.

"Yes," answered Sarah. "Yet it was me. I knew it was."

"Is that what you wish to be—a nurse?" the Mirror Man said.

Sarah nodded.

"And you'll make a wonderful nurse," the Mirror Man boomed happily. "But, now we have to be on our way."

Sarah moved down the steps of the wagon. "Where are we going?" she asked.

The Mirror Man put his hand on Look's back and patted it gently. He said, "I think that depends on you."

"On me?" asked Sarah.

The Mirror Man turned to the road. "The road goes two ways—to Whistletown and away from Whistletown. Which way do you wish to go?"

Sarah gazed longingly at the road.

"Would you like to see your family and your friends, without them knowing who you are?" the Mirror Man asked.

Sarah looked at him eagerly. "How can I do that?"

A broad smile blossomed in the Mirror Man's face. He bowed and his silk top hat tumbled from his head, down his arm and into his hand. He looked up at Sarah. "Magic," he said.

"Magic?" asked Sarah.

"Yes," the Mirror Man said in a whisper. "There's something about the Seventh Mirror I've never told anyone, Sarah. In truth, I've never seen it. But my father told me about it. He said it should only be used for very special people at very special times." He smiled warmly. "And you, Sarah, are a special person to me, and this is a special time."

"I don't understand," said Sarah.

"The person you saw in the mirror you can become for one complete day," explained the Mirror Man. He lifted a finger in front of his face. "But only one day, twenty-four hours."

"How?" asked Sarah.

"First, you must tell me if you would like to do that," answered the Mirror Man. "If you do, we will go to Whistletown and you can see for yourself how much your family and your friends miss you."

"Oh, yes," Sarah said eagerly.

"But, remember, it is only for the day. Tomorrow, at this hour, you will again be the Sarah you are now," warned the Mirror Man.

"I understand," Sarah said.

The Mirror Man knelt before Sarah and took her hands. "You must close your eyes and remember what you saw in the Seventh Mirror. See yourself again, exactly as you saw yourself in the mirror. And when you do, hold your hands above your head and snap your fingers, first with your right hand, second with your left hand, and then with both hands. He stood and closed his eyes and then slowly raised his hands above his head and snapped his fingers, right hand first, left hand second, then both hands at the same time. He opened one eye and looked down at Sarah. "Do you understand?"

"Y— Yes," Sarah answered.

"Don't be afraid," the Mirror Man said gently.

Sarah closed her eyes and imagined being in the room of the Seventh Mirror, the room of gold and yellow stars. She saw the shimmering white light and the appearance of the young woman dressed in the uniform of a nurse. Then she raised her hands above her head and snapped her fingers as the Mirror Man had instructed.

A strange sensation tingled in her body, like the warmth of the sun covering her on a cool day. She heard the Mirror Man say, "Sarah."

She opened her eyes. The Mirror Man stood before her, but not so tall as he had been. A funny, startled expression was on his face.

"Oh, my," the Mirror Man whispered.

The young woman standing before him, wearing the uniform of a nurse, was beautiful, yet she looked very much like Sarah, the child.

"Oh, my," the Mirror Man repeated. "You should see yourself." He reached into the inside pocket of his tuxedo coat and removed a small hand mirror. "Mirrors, mirrors everywhere," he said. "But this one is just a mirror mirror. There's nothing special about it. What you see is what you are." He held the mirror up for Sarah.

Sarah gazed into it.

And then she smiled.

"Are you ready to go home?" asked the Mirror Man.

"Yes," she said softly.

In mid-afternoon, from the mountain overlooking a valley of trees and fields, the Mirror Man and Sarah could see the steeple of the courthouse of Whistletown.

The courthouse was in the exact middle of the town, surrounded by stores and shops. Streets, lined with white-painted houses, led away from the town.

"Look," Sarah said excitedly. "I can see my home." She tugged at the Mirror Man's arm and pointed toward the village. "It's there, not far from the school."

The Mirror Man cupped his hand over his eyes to shade the glare of the afternoon sun. He did not know which home belonged to Sarah's family, but he pretended that he did. "Oh, yes," he said. "It's very pretty."

"It's the prettiest home in the world," Sarah said. "Why would my parents want to leave it?"

"Perhaps they don't want to leave," suggested the Mirror Man. "Perhaps it's something they must do. It's one of the things hard to understand about grown-ups, Sarah. Even grown-ups don't understand it, but sometimes you do what you must do, rather than what you would like to do. What is your father's work?"

"He's a teacher," answered Sarah.

"He's going to teach at another school, is that it?" asked the Mirror Man.

"Yes," Sarah said. "It's far away, at the university."

"He must be a very fine teacher for such an honor," said the Mirror Man.

"Yes," Sarah replied quietly.

***

When the Mirror Man and Sarah rode into Whistletown, they knew immediately something was happening. People were rushing about madly, up streets and down streets, bumping into one another like children playing a frantic game of hide-and-seek. They were led by a tall man wearing a bright red beret and carrying a large notebook. He was marching in a circle, giving orders in a rhyming, singsong voice:

"Go look again, look everywhere!

"If she's not here, she could be there!

"Look in the shops and all the stores!

"Up in the trees, behind the doors!

"Look to your left and to your right!

"In front of you and out of sight!"

The man paused, opened his book, and began to write frantically with a quill pen that he pulled from his pocket, and then he called out:

"Look everywhere there is a where!

"Then start again and go back there!"

The Mirror Man smiled. He knew the leader of the bumbling crowd as Latimer Compton Boyette, the Town Poet of Whistletown. If words were to be used for any purpose other than day-by-day speaking, the Town Poet believed only he should use them. He was, after all, a poet, and who but poets could possibly understand the deep, hidden, mysterious meanings of words? Somewhere among his collection of odd, unneeded things, the Mirror Man even had a business card that read:

Latimer Compton Boyette
Writer & Official Town Poet

The jingling harness bells of Look and See rang merrily along the street, and the people paused in their rushing about to smile and to wave to the Mirror Man and to the pretty young woman seated beside him.

"What are they doing?" asked Sarah.

"Why, they're looking for you," the Mirror Man told her as he stopped his wagon near the courthouse. A group of children quickly gathered around Look and See.

"It looks as though you already have some customers," said a shopkeeper wearing a baker's hat and an apron. "I wish I could get customers so easily." He tipped his hat to Sarah and turned and went back into his bakery shop.

A great sadness fell over Sarah. The baker was one of her favorite people in Whistletown. He made the best butter cookies in the world, and he was always happy, always glad to see her. Yet, now he did not know her.

She turned back to look at the crowd of children petting Look and See. She knew all of them. Tina and Jilian and Rachel and Melita and Roger and Philip and George. All of them were her friends.

The Mirror Man patted her hand and whispered to her, "Are you all right?"

"They're—they're my friends," Sarah answered, also in whisper.

"And they don't know who you are," said the Mirror Man. "Nor did the baker."

"No," Sarah said in a lonely voice.

"Oh, don't worry," the Mirror Man assured her. "They're still your friends. Some things never change."

Suddenly, the door to the courthouse opened and the Mayor, a short, plump man dressed in a dark blue suit with a high-collar shirt and a wide yellow tie, waddled briskly down to the sidewalk. A tall man dressed in a police chief's uniform, with his police chief's hat pulled low over his eyes, followed him.

"Arrumph," the Mayor said in his official mayor's voice. "Good day, Mirror Man."

"Good day Mr. Mayor, Mr. Chief of Police," replied the Mirror Man cheerfully. "It's a fine day, isn't it?"

"Indeed," said the Police Chief with a broad smile.

The Mayor frowned and squinted toward the sun. "Yes, yes," he said in a serious tone. "Fine enough for a fine day if it's a fine day you're wanting, but there's a heavy, dark cloud hanging over Whistletown. You can't see it, but it's there. Yes, indeed. Indeed, yes."

"And why is that?" asked the Mirror Man, climbing down from his wagon.

"One of our children is missing," the Mayor said gravely.

"Missing," said the Police Chief, shaking his head sadly.

The Town Poet hurried past, followed by a crowd of people wearing worried expressions.

"You must keep searching; do not stop!" the Town Poet bellowed, reading from his book.

"Find where she is, not where she's not!"

"...where she is, not where she's not!" the crowd echoed in unison.

"All the people of the town are looking for her," the Mayor told the Mirror Man. "Her father and some of the other men are searching the countryside. I've ordered the Town Poet to inspire our people with his words, since I can't be everywhere at the same time I am to be somewhere else."

"And why is she missing?" asked the Mirror Man.

The Mayor sighed and wagged his head in the way a mayor would do to show a heavy heart. "Her father and mother plan to move to another city, and she wants to stay in Whistletown," he said. "She left a note saying she had run away."

"So, she's not missing, she's hiding," said the Mirror Man.

The Mayor frowned. "If she's hiding, she's missing, which is the same as missing without hiding, is it not? You didn't see a young girl along the roadside, did you?"

"Girl?" said the Mirror Man. He glanced at Sarah, sitting on the wagon seat. A look of fear was on her face. "A little girl?" he added.

"Yes," said the Mayor. He leveled his hand in front of him. "About so high. Blond hair. Blue eyes."

"Well, now, you can see the only young lady around is my friend, the nurse," said the Mirror Man. "She, too, has blond hair and blue eyes, but at the moment, she's not a little girl."

The Mayor stepped closer to the wagon and looked up at Sarah. His eyebrows wiggled across his forehead. Sarah could feel a blush coloring her face. The Mayor's daughter, Tina, was one of her best friends. She was certain the Mayor recognized her.

"Arrumph. A nurse, you say?" the Mayor said.

"Indeed, a fine young nurse," the Mirror Man told him.

"Well, we have need of you," the Mayor announced.

"Sir?" said Sarah.

"The mother of our missing little girl has fallen ill with grief," the Mayor explained. "She's in the courthouse, in my office. We've been waiting for one of our doctors to arrive."

"Oh, no," Sarah said urgently. "I—can't . . . "

"And why not?" demanded the Mayor. "You're a nurse, are you not?"

"But…" Sarah said in a small voice.

"Of course she can," said the Mirror Man. He winked at Sarah, and then he turned to the Mayor. "She's only just become a nurse, you see. She still doesn't understand that she really knows what to do." He looked back at Sarah. "It's like magic," he added. "You cannot be who you are meant to be, unless you are certain of who you are."

A frown of confusion waved across the Mayor's forehead as he considered the Mirror Man's words. "Arrumph," he arrumphed in a loud voice. "Of course that's true. True enough, indeed. I've said so many times in many of my finer speeches. Come along now. Come along."

"Come along," the Police Chief echoed.

And so Sarah went with the Mayor and the Police Chief and the Mirror Man into the courthouse, and there, in the mayor's office, she found her mother huddled in a large, lean-back chair, her eyes closed, a weary expression covering her face. Across her lap, was a blanket she had woven for Sarah when Sarah was a baby.

"I see she's finally fallen asleep," the Mayor said quietly.

"She was awake all night," whispered the Police Chief.

"Then she needs rest," suggested the Mirror Man.

"True enough," said the Mayor. "Now, young lady, we'll leave you to tend to your patient, and we'll join the others searching for our missing little girl."

***

Sarah looked fearfully at the Mirror Man.

"You'll be fine," the Mirror Man assured her. "You'll know what to do." He smiled. "Remember, you're a nurse."

"Come, come," said the Mayor, waving his chubby hands. "There's work to do, no time to waste."

The Mirror Man smiled at Sarah and winked once more, and then he followed the Mayor and the Police Chief out of the courthouse.

Sarah stood beside the chair where her mother slept. She had never seen her mother look so tired.

"I'm so sorry," she said softly.

She touched her mother's forehead. It was fever hot.

A worry fever, she thought.

She remembered having such a fever when she was very small, just before Christmas. Her mother had bathed her face with a cool, damp cloth and had sung lullabies to her. "You only have a worry fever," her mother had said. "A worry fever that Christmas won't be here fast enough."

She knew that her mother's worry fever was because of her.

She looked around the mayor's office. On a table behind his large desk, she saw a pitcher of water and a basin, and beside the basin, was a hand towel.

She thought of the words of the Mirror Man: "You'll know what to do. Remember, you're a nurse."

"Yes," she whispered. She did know what to do. A worry fever only needed love.

As Sarah, the nurse, cared for her mother, the Mayor and the Police Chief and the Mirror Man joined the Town Poet and the citizens of Whistletown in their search for Sarah, the child.

"Mirror Man," said the Mayor, "if you were a child and wanted to run away, where would you go?"

The Mirror Man tilted his head as though listening to the question a second time, and then he said, "It has been too many years since I was a child to think as a child would think. But it's a good question. Perhaps we should ask the children."

"Of course," the Mayor replied. "Yes, indeed. Indeed, yes. It was my very thinking. I simply wanted to rehearse the question before I posed it to them." He turned to the Police Chief. "Gather the children," he instructed.

***

Suddenly, from the far end of Whistletown, a large truck, billowing steam from its engine, rolled noisily down the street and came to a shuddering stop in front of the Mayor and the Police Chief and the Mirror Man.

The Mayor scurried quickly behind the Police Chief, then peered around him to see a tall, heavy man step from the truck. The man had a long, dark beard and thick, dark hair that curled over his shoulders. He wore an eye patch over his left eye, and the hat on his head was rolled at the brim like the hat of a seaman. A sneer crowded his face and an evil smile curled across his mouth. He spoke in a rumbling, ill-tempered voice: "Me name be Jake the Hunter. There be word about that you be missing a child."

The Mirror Man frowned. He knew of the man named Jake the Hunter – a former pirate from the ocean town of Hightide and a man not to be trusted, for a pirate on the sea is also a pirate on land.

"True enough," the Mirror Man said. "As you can see, the entire town's looking for her."

"And have you seen such a child?" the Mayor asked anxiously from behind the Police Chief.

"Would I be asking about her if I had?" growled Jake the Hunter. He turned to the truck and snapped his fingers, and a bony, black dog rose up menacingly from the front seat. It had the fierce features of a hungry wolf, with narrow, piercing eyes and short, pointed ears. It opened its mouth and snarled, and a row of white, sharp teeth flashed in the sun.

"Oh, my," whispered the Mayor fearfully.

"This be Sniffer," crowed Jake the Hunter. "He be the finest tracking dog in all the country. Why, if you lost a thought you was having, he'd be finding it before you knew it was gone. It's him that'll find your girl."

"He must be a very fine dog," said the Mirror Man.

"Aye, that he is," said Jake the Hunter. "We've hunted down everything from squirrels to scalawags, goblins to ghosts. It be lost, the Sniffer will be finding it." He paused and smiled. "For a price, of course," he added in his silky, teasing voice.

"Ah, a price," said the Mirror Man. "And what would that price be?"

Jake the Hunter reached to rub Sniffer across his head. "Seeing it's a small girl—helpless as she must be—and seeing her being missing has caused such a worry, it'll be a bit more costly than the normal finding-a-person fee might be."

"Of course," said the Mirror Man. "Somehow, I thought that would be your answer. But you still didn't give an amount."

Jake the Hunter tilted his head to look at the Mayor with his one good eye. "The fee will be— " He paused and listened to the sound of panic in the voice of the Town Poet, who was nearby, still urging the citizens of Whistletown to keep searching for Sarah.

"Did you look there, or there, or there?" the Town Poet demanded.

"Keep on the watch with careful care!

"We must find her, we really must!

"She's all alone, we're lots of us!"

Jake the Hunter's smile eased again across his dark face. "The fee will be ten thousand kronons," he hissed.

The Mayor gasped. He reached into his coat pocket and withdrew a handkerchief and dabbed it across his brow. "Arrrrrump," he exclaimed. "Ten thousand kronons? Impossible. There's not ten thousand kronons in all of Whistletown."

"Not at all. Oh, no," sputtered the Police Chief. "Ten thousand kronons? Never. Never. Oh, no."

"And what sort of men be you?" snapped Jake the Hunter. "You'd let a small girl go missing for the sake of money?"

The Mayor poked his head around the Police Chief, a flush of anger on his face. "Of course not," he said forcefully, "it's just that – "

"You be a sorry lot," roared Jake the Hunter. The Sniffer arched his back and the hair on his neck stood up. He lowered his head and narrowed his eyes and glared at the Mayor. A low growl rumbled in his throat.

"Oh, my. Oh, my," stammered the Mayor, trembling. He ducked back behind the Police Chief.

"Excuse me, friend," said the Mirror Man in his pleasant manner, "I think there's been a misunderstanding. Of course, the missing girl is worth ten thousand kronons. Every child in every place on all the Earth is worth ten thousand kronons, then another ten thousand, and another, until all the kronons ever made are counted for."

Jake the Hunter turned to face the Mirror Man. He squinted his good eye suspiciously. "Aye, you be right," he said. "And I be asking only for the first ten thousand."

The Mirror Man stepped forward, toward Jake the Hunter. "Do you see that fine wagon and the two grand white horses tethered to the post, there across the street?" he asked.

Jake the Hunter twisted to look in the direction of the Mirror Man's gesture. "Aye," he said. "They be yours?"

"Indeed, they are," answered the Mirror Man. "It's a wagon of trick mirrors. I travel across the country entertaining children with it. It has been in my family for more than a century."

"And what has that to do with me?" demanded Jake the Hunter

"I've a bargain for you," said the Mirror Man. "My horses and wagon are far more valuable than ten thousand kronons. I will offer them to you if you and your splendid animal find the child." He paused. "However, if you fail to do so before the sun goes dim beyond the hills, you will vow to leave Whistletown and not return."

Suddenly, from the steeple of the courthouse, the whistle of Whistletown whistled, signaling the five-o'clock hour. Sniffer lifted his head and howled mournfully:

Arrrrrrrrrrrrroooooooooooo....

"Five o'clock," said the Mirror Man cheerfully. "There's little time left before the sun falls. Perhaps it is an unfair bargain."

Jake the Hunter furrowed his brow in thought. He stroked his beard with his fingers. "Agreed," he said after a moment. "I know an old sea mate who could use the wagon for carrying fish to market and would gladly pay handsome for it, and the horses look strong enough for field work. The two of them would be fetching a fancy price."

Sadness struck the Mirror Man. It was painful to think of Look and See being used as plough horses, or of his magic wagon carting fish from shop to shop. Still, Jake the Hunter's demand of ten thousand kronons was much the same as robbery, and he could not permit that to happen to the people of Whistletown.

Yet, he also knew Look and See and his wagon were safe. The bargain was for Sniffer to find the child Sarah, *not the adult Sarah,* and at that moment—

because of the magic of the Seventh Mirror—Sarah was an adult.

"Then we have an agreement," said the Mirror Man.

"Aye, we do," said Jake the Hunter.

"But, but – " stammered the Mayor to the Mirror Man, "your wagon, your fine horses…"

"A small price for a small girl," said the Mirror Man, smiling.

Jake the Hunter snapped his fingers and Sniffer leapt from the truck to the ground. He lifted his head and bayed loudly—Arrrrrrrrrrrrroooooooooooo… —and the baying echoed, causing the Whistletownians of Whistletown to stop their rushing about in search of Sarah.

"Fetch me a thing belonging to the child," bellowed Jake the Hunter.

"Yes, of course, a thing," said the Mayor. He gave a puzzled look to the Mirror Man.

"Perhaps her mother would have something," the Mirror Man suggested.

"Yes, yes, I was about to say that," agreed the Mayor. "Indeed, I was. The words were making their way out of my mouth when you spoke up." Then, to the Police Chief, he said, "Go, go, ask the mother."

The Mirror Man stepped forward. He made a slight, courteous bow to the Mayor. "Permit me, Your Honor," he said. "I see the crowd is beginning to gather round. Perhaps the Police Chief should stay here to help you keep control."

The Mayor glanced again at Jake the Hunter. Jake the Hunter glared at him with a menacing stare.

"A fine idea," said the Mayor. "I was thinking the same, just as you said it, Mirror Man. We think alike, the two of us. You would make a fine mayor."

The Mirror Man smiled. "You're kind," he said to the Mayor, "but it takes a special man to be a mayor, one who knows how to keep order, and I see only one such man in this company."

"Arrrumph," said the Mayor, blushing from the compliment. He turned to the assembling crowd. "Stay back! Stay back!" he commanded. "Order! Order! We must have order."

"Order! Order!" cried the Police Chief.

"Order! Order!" echoed the Town Poet.

The Mayor turned back to the Mirror Man. "Off with you, then," he said in his official mayor's voice. "Off, off."

"Off, off," added the Police Chief.

"Off, off," exclaimed the Town Poet.

In the mayor's office, Sarah paced nervously, constantly checking on her mother and going to the window to watch the rushing about of the townspeople of Whistletown, all of them searching for her, not knowing she was there among them, not as the child they were seeking, but as the adult she would become.

She wondered about the old truck that had shuddered to a stop near the Mayor and the Police Chief and the Mirror Man and the Town Poet. She wondered about the mean-faced man who stepped from the truck, and the fierce-looking dog that stood beside him. She wondered why the Mirror Man had started walking leisurely toward the courthouse, circled by a crowd of children who were her friends.

Has he told them who I am? she wondered.

There were so many questions, so much to think about, that she began to feel dizzy.

She turned to her mother, still sleeping in the Mayor's lean-back chair, the look of worry still resting in her face. She whispered again, "I'm so sorry, Mother. I'm so sorry."

She heard footsteps in the corridor outside the mayor's office, followed by the noise of voices saying words too distant to understand, and then the door to the office opened slowly and the Mirror Man stepped inside, closing the door quickly behind him. He smiled and bowed to Sarah, then he pointed to Sarah's mother and said in the mouthing of words, but not with sound, "How is she?"

"Still asleep," said Sarah, also mouthing the words.

"Good," said the Mirror Man, aloud, but quietly. He crossed the room to Sarah.

"What's happening?" Sarah asked frightfully. "Why is everyone standing by that old truck? Who is that terrible-looking man with that scary-looking dog?"

"You are not to worry," answered the Mirror Man. "He calls himself Jake the Hunter. Once, he was a pirate sailing the seven seas and plundering every ship that crossed in his path."

"A pirate?" Sarah said in an astonished voice.

"That is true. Long ago, before he became seasick," explained the Mirror Man. "Now he's a pirate on land, but a pirate is a pirate wherever he is. Now he goes about the countryside with his dog, Sniffer, finding things that people have lost."

"Why is he here?" asked Sarah.

The Mirror Man smiled. "To find you," he answered. "And he wants a fortune in kronons to do it."

"Oh," gasped Sarah. "We have no money."

"And you'll have no need of it," promised the Mirror Man. He glanced out the window and smiled at the sight of the Mayor hiding behind the Police Chief, while Jake the Hunter sneered at the crowd that had gathered nearby, and then he turned back to Sarah. "We have a bargain," he said. "He will be seeking the child, not the grown-up, and you, dear Sarah, are not a child. Not in this moment." He reached inside his coat pocket and removed his small hand mirror and held it up to Sarah. "Remember?" he whispered. "Magic."

Sarah gazed at her image. It was still startling to see herself as an adult. She touched her face with her fingers.

"Who is that, that Who I see?" the Mirror Man sang in a soft voice. "Is it it, or is it me?"

Sarah smiled. "Me," she said. "Yes, me."

The Mirror Man slipped the mirror back into his pocket and smiled again and did his funny face, the same one he made in showing Sarah the mirrors in his wagon. "Now I need a garment, or something you would have touched," he added. "Something for the search." He paused. "Do you understand?" he asked gently.

Sarah's face became suddenly bright. Of course, she thought. The Mirror Man was playing a great game. "Yes," she said excitedly. "My mother has one of the blankets she made for me when I was a baby. You can use that."

***

And so the Mirror Man took the blanket and carried it to Jake the Hunter, and Jake the Hunter held it in front of Sniffer, his wolf-like dog. "Sniff it good," Jake the Hunter hissed. "You'll be finding the girl what goes with the blanket, or you'll be eating bugs for your supper."

Sniffer rubbed his face against the blanket and smiled a dog smile, one that crawled over his curled lips and up his face and settled like a light in his narrow eyes. He lowered his head and began to sniff, and then he lifted his head and bayed,

Arrrrrrrrrrrrroooooooooooo...

"He's got it," roared Jake the Hunter. He thrust his face toward the Mirror Man. "The wagon's mine to be having, matey," he sneered. "And them horses, and all that goes with them. You've lost the bargain, you have." He waved his arms at the crowd and bellowed, "Ahoy, there, you landlubbers, step aside, step aside!" He snapped his fingers over Sniffer's head, and Sniffer began to trot in circles. Every few feet, he stopped and lifted his head and bayed,

Arrrrrrrrrrrrroooooooooooo…

"Oh me, oh my, oh my, oh me," the Town Poet sang out, reading from his notebook.

"What is it now that we will see?"

A small ripple of awkward applause ran through the crowd surrounding him and the Town Poet bowed proudly.

To the Mirror Man, it was much the same as watching street comedy by a touring group of actors – Sniffer, the dog, leading the way, sniffing the ground and baying, Jake the Hunter close behind, roaring like the bully that he was, followed by the Police Chief, marching in step with Jake the Hunter, and the Mayor trailing the Police Chief, arrumphing in his mayor's voice. And following along, step by step, were the Town Poet and the townspeople, the Whistletownians of Whistletown, making the search for Sarah, the child, appear to be a dance to the music of Arrrrrrrrrrrrroooooooooooo… and "Arrumph…"

Arrrrrrrrrrrrroooooooooooo…

Step, step, step.

"Arrumph…"

Step, step, step.

Arrrrrrrrrrrrroooooooooooo…

Step, step, step.

"Arrumph…"

Step, step, step.

Sniffer sniffed the streets, up and down. He sniffed in the doorway of the grocer and the baker, sniffed at the windows of the dress shop and the candy-cane maker. He sniffed and sniffed at the shop of toys, sniffed at the girls, sniffed at the boys.

Arrrrrrrrrrrrooooooooooo…

Arrrrrrrrrrrrooooooooooo…

"Arrumph…"

"Arrumph…"

And then Sniffer came to the Mirror Man's wagon. He sniffed once, twice, three times. He lifted his head and sniffed the air in a deep, long breath. Then he looked at Jake the Hunter and smiled his dog smile. His sharp, white teeth glistened in the sunlight. He opened his mouth and bayed in a voice so loud it caused the townspeople of Whistletown to leap back in fear:

Arrrrrrrrrrrroooooooooooooooooooooooooo…

"She be here, in the wagon," thundered Jake the Hunter. He turned to the Mirror Man. "Open the door, or I'll be smashing it in," he ordered.

"No reason for that," said the Mirror Man. "The door's unlocked. You're welcome to search—if you're careful not to break the mirrors."

Jake the Hunter leaned close to the Mirror Man. "It's not mirrors I'll be breaking if you be hiding the girl," he snarled. Then he pushed Sniffer aside with his foot. "Stay, you mangy mutt," he ordered. He tugged at his pirate's hat and slowly, cautiously mounted the steps to the Mirror Man's wagon.

***

Inside the wagon, Jake the Hunter paused. He blinked his good eye and shook his head. How could this be? he wondered. From outside, the wagon seemed too small for him to stand upright, yet, now—inside—it was as large as a ship's hull. He glared at the high ceiling, painted sky blue, with the painted sun peeking from behind painted clouds, and for a moment, he thought he was again on some sea with nothing but sky covering him.

And then he saw the curtains lining both sides of the wagon.

"Would you be hiding behind them curtains, now?" he said in an evil whisper. "Little good it'll do you. Not with old Jake's good eye spying for you."

He reached for the gold braided curtain cords that operated the curtains and yanked them, sliding the curtains down the brass rods.

A scowl stole across his face.

Nothing was behind the curtains but mirrors.

He began to slink forward. "All right, little girlie, come out, come out," he said in a sweet, teasing voice. "Come see your old friend, Jake. I'll be showing you me gold ring, I will. Belonged to a prince. A fine man, he was. Give it to me as a be-gone gift." He laughed again, softly. "His ring for me to be gone."

He took three long steps to the middle of the wagon, and did a quick full turn. Suddenly, he saw a crowd of crazed, distorted people surrounding him, and he began to jump around, swinging wildly, bewildered that the images swinging back at him—some fat and squat, some tall and thin—all had the look of pirates wearing an eye patch.

And then he realized the images he saw were reflections of himself in the Mirror Man's mirrors, and a sour, embarrassed look passed like a shadow across his face. He leaned to his left and saw his image melt from one mirror into another, like a ghost changing shapes. He leaned to his right and saw his arms stretch out like a rope. "Ha!" he snorted. Then he moved from mirror to mirror, watching his image wiggle into such odd shapes that his good eye had trouble seeing everything.

A trick, he thought. A trick of mirrors. Aye, that was it. And that would make the wagon worth even more than he had imagined. "You're a shrewd one, Jake," he said to himself. He cackled a laugh. "A shrewd one," he repeated.

Still, he did not have time for entertainment. Merriment would come later—a party for his old shipmates—when he owned the wagon, but to own the wagon, he had to find the girl.

"Come out, come out," he whispered, still in his sweet, teasing voice. "I'll not harm you. You have me promise on it. Why, I'll go to the candy-cane shop and buy you a treat, a lollipop, one the size of a coffee saucer."

He paused and listened. He heard nothing.

"I know you be hiding," he growled. "And where would you be?"

He peered around the wagon room and saw the door near the front of the wagon. He crept forward. A sign on the door read:

FOR CHILDREN ONLY

"So, that's where you are, is it?" said Jake the Hunter. "Hiding behind your own special door, are you? Ha! Not for long."

He grabbed the handle of the door and twisted it and yanked open the door, and then he dropped into a squat and stretched his arms to catch whoever might be trying to escape. "Gotcha," he roared, swiping his arms together. But his arms were empty of everything except air. He did not see anyone. He saw only a mirror. Not a mirror like those along the walls of the wagon, but a mirror that could be seen in any shop or home—a dressing mirror, tall and narrow and flat. Yet, there was something different about it. He stood and moved closer, bending forward, squinting at the mirror through his good eye. A light seemed to shimmer in the face of the mirror, and Jake the Hunter saw his image quiver, then slowly change. He stepped back, puzzled. The image staring at him was that of a knight in a gleaming suit of armor. He felt a tremor flutter in his chest, and an ancient memory came flooding back: as a child, he had wanted to be a knight.

He reached for the door and closed it quickly and leaned against it. He could feel his face becoming pale and cool. He tried to walk, but his legs were wobbly. He closed his good eye and shook his head, yet he could not push the image of the knight from his seeing.

Then he snarled and slapped at his face with the palm of his hand. "Avast," he growled. "I be who I be. Not a knight. Them was child's wishes."

He whirled and marched down the center of the wagon, not giving a look to the mirrors as he passed them. At the back of the wagon, he turned and glared at the door bearing the sign:

FOR CHILDREN ONLY

"You've been here," he said in an angry whisper. "I can feel you, crawling on me skin. I'll find you. I'll find you, sure as me name be Jake the Hunter."

Watching from the window of the mayor's office in the courthouse, Sarah saw Jake the Hunter stalk down the steps of the Mirror Man's wagon, waving his arms and shouting angrily. She could almost hear his words in the faraway roar of his voice, and a sudden chill raced across her shoulders. She wanted to cry out for her mother, but she knew her mother was still sleeping from her worry fever.

She watched the ferocious-looking dog named Sniffer, with his nose close to the ground, sniffing, and she could hear his baying getting closer and closer and closer.

Arrrrrrrrrrrrrroooooooooooo…

Arrrrrrrrrrrrrroooooooooooo…

Arrrrrrrrrrrrroooooooooooo...

Arrrrrrrrrrrrroooooooooooo...

Following behind the dog, she saw the terrible man named Jake the Hunter, and behind Jake the Hunter, she saw the Police Chief and the Mayor and the Mirror Man and the Town Poet and all the people of Whistletown. They were heading toward the courthouse.

And then she heard a sound behind her and she turned to see her mother sitting forward in her chair, staring curiously at Sarah.

"Who are you?" asked her mother.

"I—I'm a nurse," Sarah said hesitantly. She moved to her mother's chair and took the damp face towel from its basin and began to pat her mother's face with it.

"A nurse?" questioned her mother. "You look familiar, but I've never seen you and I know everyone in Whistletown."

"I'm—just visiting," Sarah said. "The Mayor asked me to sit with you."

"Have they found my little girl?" her mother asked anxiously.

"Not yet," Sarah told her. "But they will. I'm sure of it."

Her mother began to weep quietly.

"Please don't," begged Sarah. "She's fine. I promise you she is."

"Do you know why she left?" asked her mother.

Sarah wiped her mother's eyes with the damp cloth. "Yes," she answered. "They told me."

"We don't want to leave Whistletown either, but sometimes you must do what you'd rather not do," her mother said. She looked up at Sarah. "Did you not leave your home to become a nurse?"

The question startled Sarah. She thought: Yes, to become a nurse, I would have to leave Whistletown. And that was what the Mirror Man meant when he said, "Sometimes you do what you must do, rather than what you would like to do."

"Did you?" said her mother. "Did you have to leave home?"

"Why—why, yes," answered Sarah.

"But if I could see her now, I would tell her that if she wanted to stay, we would never leave Whistletown," said her mother.

"Maybe she doesn't feel that way any longer," Sarah said softly.

Her mother began to weep again. "I just want to see her."

A great wave of regret and sorrow swept over Sarah. She kneeled before her mother and took her hands. "I have something to tell you," she said, but before she could speak again, the door to the mayor's office flew open and the doorway was filled with

Sniffer, the sniffing dog, and with Jake the Hunter and with the Mirror Man and the Mayor and the Police Chief and the Town Poet, who was writing furiously in his notebook.

Arrrrrrrrrrrrroooooooooooo... bayed Sniffer, and the baying echoed like the roaring of a great windstorm, causing Sarah's mother to cry out and to cover her face with her hands.

Sarah jumped to her feet and stood between Sniffer and her mother.

"There she be!" cried Jake the Hunter as Sniffer bounced to Sarah, sniffing madly, dancing in circles, baying, prancing proudly.

"Where?" said the Mirror Man.

Jake the Hunter jabbed a finger toward Sarah. "There!" he bellowed again.

"Oh," said the Mirror Man, crossing the room to Sarah. "You mean this young lady, the Nurse?"

A look of confusion burrowed into Jake the Hunter's face. He leaned forward and squinted his good eye toward Sarah.

"I believe the missing child is—well, a child," said the Mirror Man over the baying of Sniffer. "As you can surely see, this young lady is not a child."

"Not a child," the Police Chief echoed with authority.

"Indeed, no." emphasized the Mayor from behind the Police Chief. He added a distinctive and mayoral, "Arrumph."

Again, Sniffer bayed, Arrrrrrrrrrrroooooooo… and Sarah's mother gasped in fear. She reached for Sarah's hand and held it tightly.

"I'm afraid your fine animal is alarming the ladies," the Mirror Man said to Jake the Hunter. "Could you quiet him?"

Jake the Hunter growled irritably and snapped his fingers. "Belay your yelping, you fleabag," he snapped, and Sniffer immediately quit his baying and dropped to the floor, cowering under the lashing tone of his master.

The room fell silent except for the worried breathing of Sarah's mother. Jake the Hunter took a long step forward, toward Sarah. He studied her with his good eye. "A nurse, are you?" he said.

"Y—yes," answered Sarah. She looked nervously at the Mirror Man.

"And have you treated a small girl?" Jake the Hunter pressed.

Sarah shook her head. She squeezed her mother's hand.

"But you be carrying the scent of her," said Jake the Hunter. "Or me dog's lost what his nose knows."

The Mirror Man leaned over to pat Sniffer on his head. "I think I can answer that," he said. "It's because your prize animal has become too good at his work."

"Bah," rumbled Jake the Hunter. "Not good enough, you mean. He'll find himself on the side of the road, howling at the moon before this day's done."

"Well, do as you must," said the Mirror Man. "But perhaps you would be making a grave error in judgment."

"And what makes you say such a thing?" snapped Jake the Hunter.

"Think about it," said the Mirror Man. "You wanted a garment, or something the girl would have touched, is that not right?"

"Aye," mumbled Jake the Hunter.

The Mirror Man began to pace around the room, as a man will do when he is in deep thought. "And I volunteered to come to the courthouse—here, in this room—to inquire if her mother had such an item," he said.

"And so?" Jake the Hunter demanded. The Mirror Man paused in his pacing. He furrowed his brow and nodded his head as if agreeing with whatever thought had settled in his mind. Then he said, "The girl's mother, who is now awake, but was then asleep—" he bowed slightly to Sarah's mother—"was there in her chair." He paused again. "The Mayor's chair, of course." He dipped his head in a bow to acknowledge the Mayor and the Mayor bowed in response.

The Mirror Man began pacing again. "I spoke to the Nurse," he said, dipping his head to Sarah, "about the need for having something the missing girl would have touched, and she reasoned that the child's blanket held by the sleeping mother"—he again nodded to Sarah's mother—"would serve such a purpose. Thus, she took it from the child's mother and handed it to me." He paused and smiled triumphantly at Jake the Hunter. "And that is why your fine animal has made such a fuss over the Nurse, because she had touched the blanket."

Jake the Hunter shifted his one-eyed gaze from the Mirror Man to Sniffer, then from Sniffer back to the Mirror Man. A look of confusion clouded his face. "Avast, matey," he snarled. "You be holding the blanket as well, and there's been no barking or no sniffing of you. Now why would that be?"

The Mirror Man's smile faded. He knew he had to think fast to answer Jake the Hunter's very sensible question. "Indeed," he said after a moment. "Of course. Indeed, indeed, indeed." He kneeled again to pat Sniffer on the head. Then he added, "The answer is simple: she's a young lady; I'm a man, long in his years."

Jake the Hunter rubbed his beard. He swiveled his head from Sarah to the Mirror Man. "And what be the difference?" he said darkly. "Skin be skin, and what holds on one is the same as what holds on another."

The Mirror Man stood. "So it would seem, but there's a world of difference between what is seemed to be and what is," he declared in a spirited voice.

"What man do you know that carries such a sweet scent as that of a lovely young lady? Why, none."

"None," exclaimed the Mayor.

"None," added the Town Poet, waving his quill pen in the air.

"I'm sure your fine animal is only confused," said the Mirror Man to Jake the Hunter. He glanced out of the window of the mayor's office. "And as I see it, the day is nearing its end," he added. "If the child is not here, in this room, then perhaps she is somewhere else in the town." He paused. "I believe our bargain ends at day's end."

A flash of worry wiggled across Jake the Hunter's face. He snapped his fingers over Sniffer's head. "Up, you worthless hound," he growled.

Sniffer rose slowly from the floor. He looked fearfully at Jake the Hunter, then turned his eyes back to Sarah. He sniffed once, long and deep. A low growl trembled in his throat.

"Begone with you," Jake the Hunter commanded, stalking to the door of the mayor's office and opening it. Sniffer followed him, the low growl still trembling in his throat. At the door he turned to look at Sarah. His growl became a whimper, and a soft, sad expression blinked in his eyes.

"Out, out," snapped Jake the Hunter, and Sniffer trotted through the door, with Jake the Hunter trailing, followed by the Police Chief and the Mayor and the Town Poet. The Mirror Man made his funny, wobbly dance step to the door. He turned and bowed to Sarah, then stepped through the doorway, closing the door behind him.

Outside, the sun rested on the horizon, its rays coating Whistletown in soft hues of gold and amber and orange. For the Mirror Man, it had been a perfect day—bright, colorful, invigorating, a breeze that was cool, but not cold, warm, but not hot. The scent of flowers perfumed the breeze. Birds were chirping happily.

The Mirror Man smiled. Soon the sun would snuggle into the purple quilt of night and burrow its face in the dark pillow of the mountains and the bargain with Jake the Hunter would be over.

He watched as the crowd scurried about in its hunt for Sarah.

Arrrrrrrrrrrrroooooooooooo, bayed Sniffer.

"Arrumph," arrumphed the Mayor.

Step, step, step.

The Mirror Man reached into his coat pocket and removed his flute. He began to play cheerfully, and then he did a quick march-step to join the crowd.

Up the street, the crowd moved, following Sniffer.

Step, step, step.

Arrrrrrrrrrrrroooooooooooo…

"Arrumph…"

Then, slowly, a curtain of clouds closed over the drooping sun and the first pale shadows of night seeped across the town. At the far end of Main Street, a lamplighter, carrying his long lamplighter's pole, began to ignite the town's row of streetlights.

The Mayor stepped out from behind the Police Chief. "I now declare it to be sundown in the township of Whistletown—truly and officially," he intoned in his mayor's voice.

"Belie that," roared Jake the Hunter. "There still be light enough to see. On with the hunt."

"But that wasn't the bargain, now was it?" said the Mirror Man in his pleasant manner. "Sundown means when the sun is down, not when it still casts some light against the sky, and I believe, good sir, that the sun is down enough not to be seen, not even by the Police Chief, as tall as he is."

"That is so," said the Police Chief, standing on tiptoe to search the western sky. "I cannot see even the rim of it."

"Then it is done," declared the Mayor. He stepped cautiously toward Jake the Hunter, yet staying close to the Police Chief. "Off with you," he ordered.

"Off with you. Away, away," said the Police Chief in a loud voice.

A burst of applause erupted from the townspeople of Whistletown, and the Police Chief smiled and bowed.

Jake the Hunter glared at the Mirror Man. "There be trickery here," he snarled.

"Or magic," said the Mirror Man, smiling warmly.

"Bah!" roared Jake the Hunter. He shoved past the Mirror Man and began an angry march to his truck. Sniffer, the dog, lowered his head and slowly began to follow. A soft whimper rose from his throat, causing Jake the Hunter to stop in his stride and to turn back. "Stay, you worthless fleabag," he snapped. "There be no place for the likes of you with Jake the Hunter."

Sniffer slumped to the ground and whimpered, covering his face with his front paws. He did not see Jake the Hunter drive away in a clattering of metal and a cloud of dark smoke.

"So now, you need a new home," the Mirror Man said, kneeling to pat Sniffer's head. "I think you would make a fine companion for Look and See."

"A very good thought," said the Mayor. "Indeed. I was about to suggest the same thing. That way, there would be no reason to call the Dog Catcher."

"The Dog Catcher?" said the Police Chief in a puzzled voice.

"If we had one, of course," replied the Mayor.

The Mirror Man stood and looked toward the courthouse. He thought he could see Sarah standing behind the window. "But we still have a young girl to find," he said.

"Yes, yes, of course," agreed the Mayor. He turned to the crowd and waved his hands, "Off, off," he commanded. "Find the girl, find the girl."

"We've looked everywhere," said one of the searchers. "She's not to be found."

"Look again," the Mayor ordered.

"Look again," insisted the Police Chief.

"I'm sure she's close by," said the Mirror Man with a knowing smile.

And the people of Whistletown scurried about, the singsong of the Town Poet's voice echoing along the darkening streets:

"Search every house and every shop.

"Let no one dally, no one stop.

"She's here or there or there or here.

"She's somewhere far or somewhere near.

"Look high and low and low and high.

"We're sure to find her by and by."

The Mayor began to pace in a circle on the lawn of the courthouse. "Arrumph, arrumph," he muttered with each step. He stopped suddenly and looked to his left. Then he began to pace again. "Arrumph, arrumph." He stopped again, and looked to his right. He looked up into the sky. He leaned over and picked up a leaf and looked under it.

The Police Chief also picked up a leaf and looked under it.

"I have an idea," said the Mirror Man.

"An idea?" asked the Mayor.

"Perhaps I should open my wagon of mirrors," answered the Mirror Man.

The Mayor frowned. "We have no time for such folly, Mirror Man," he said gruffly. "One of our children is missing."

"But what if she heard the merriment and became curious about it, and then came out of her hiding?" said the Mirror Man.

The Mayor wiggled his eyebrows in thought. Perhaps the Mirror Man was right. Indeed, there was something special about the house of mirrors. He remembered the first time he had looked into the mirrors as a young boy. There were nights he had even dreamed about it, dreamed that in one of the mirrors he had seen himself as the Mayor. But, of course, that was impossible, a foolish trick of foolish mirrors.

"Arrumph," the Mayor said. "Odd that you would mention such an idea, Mirror Man. I was about to say the same thing. Indeed, before you spoke, I was about to make the exact same suggestion."

"It's a very fine idea, Mr. Mayor," said the Mirror Man. "I'm glad you thought of it."

"You thought of it also, Mirror Man," replied the Mayor. "Almost at the same time as I did."

"Only almost, however," said the Mirror Man.

"Well, of course," muttered the Mayor. He clapped his hands and called out, "Arrumph! Arrumph!" and the crowd scurrying around him stopped scurrying and became quiet.

"I have had a very fine idea," the Mayor announced. "As Mayor, I declare a break from the searching and I further declare the wagon of mirrors to be opened."

Inside the mayor's office, Sarah stood at the window and watched the people of Whistletown cross the street to the Mirror Man's wagon. She could hear the merriment of the voices of her friends and the music of the Mirror Man's flute as he played his happy tune.

"What is that music?" asked her mother. "I've heard it before, but I don't remember where or when."

Sarah could see her friends crowding around the Mirror Man's wagon of mirrors. "It's the Mirror Man," she said. "He's playing his flute."

"Yes, of course," said her mother. "It's been many years since he's been in Whistle Town, but when he does come, I hear his music. Of course, his wagon is for children and it's been a long time since I was a child. I do remember his mirrors, though, and how happy I was being in his wagon."

Sarah turned to her mother. "You looked into his mirrors?" she asked with surprise.

Her mother smiled softly. "Yes," she answered. "Once. When I was younger."

"All of the mirrors?" asked Sarah.

"I think so," said her mother.

"What did you see?" questioned Sarah.

"Funny things," answered her mother. "All kinds of shapes. All so funny. I remember how we laughed. But there was one mirror —"

"The Seventh Mirror?" said Sarah.

"Yes, I believe it was," replied her mother. "One mirror in a room by itself. A very common mirror in a very pretty room."

"And what did you see in the Seventh Mirror?" asked Sarah.

Her mother moved from the chair and crossed the mayor's office to the window. She said, "I don't remember. Strange, but I don't remember."

Sarah could see the Mirror Man leading her friends to the wagon of mirrors and she could hear him singing merrily:

"Who is that, that Who I see?

"Is it it, or is it me?

"Let me lead you by the hand.

"I'm the mirrors' Mirror Man."

Sarah could feel sadness flooding over her. She turned to her mother. "I'm sorry," she said, "but I must leave now."

Her mother reached for her hand and patted it tenderly. "Thank you," she said. "I feel so much better."

"It was just a worry fever," said Sarah.

Her mother looked at her with a puzzled expression. "Why, yes, that's what it was. I used to tell my daughter that she had worry fevers when she became ill." She paused, then said, "It's strange, but you make me think of my daughter."

Sarah smiled at her mother, then turned and rushed from the mayor's office and out of the courthouse. She no longer wanted to be Sarah the Nurse. She wanted to be Sarah. Just Sarah. She wanted to be home with her mother and father, wherever that home would be.

When Sarah arrived at the wagon house of mirrors, she saw the Mirror Man standing at the red door, playing his flute, guiding a long line of waiting children into the wagon.

"Come along," called the Mirror Man happily.

And one by one, the children entered the wagon.

"How can so many children fit into such a small wagon?" said the grown-ups in amazement.

"Magic," Sarah whispered to herself. She wandered among the crowd gathered at the wagon, listening to their familiar voices. She knew everyone there, but no one recognized her. She was a stranger among them. Still, they spoke kindly to her, and she remembered what the Mirror Man said to her at the campsite: "Strangers are merely friends I haven't yet met."

She watched as the children exited the wagon laughing gleefully. She stood alone under a large elm tree on the lawn of the courthouse and watched families wandering off to their homes, and she longed to be in her own home. Far down the street, she saw her father and a group of other men returning from searching for her in the fields and woods surrounding the town.

"You look sad," said the Mirror Man, startling her. He had a wide smile on his face.

"Oh, Mirror Man," Sarah said desperately. "I want to be me again."

"You are you," the Mirror Man told her. "A grown-up you. For one day. And that day ends tomorrow morning."

"No," replied Sarah. "I'm the me who's going to be, but I'm not the me I want to be."

The Mirror Man frowned seriously. "Ummmm," he said. "I think I know what to do. Come with me."

And Sarah followed the Mirror Man into the house of mirrors, to the door of the Seventh Mirror.

"Go look into the Seventh Mirror, Sarah," the Mirror Man said. "Think of yourself as you were as a little girl. Wish to be that girl, and when you see her, raise your hands above your head and snap your fingers as you did before."

Sarah did as the Mirror Man instructed. Inside the room of the Seventh Mirror, she closed her eyes and imagined herself as a little girl. And then she opened her eyes and stared into the mirror. She saw a bright, blinding white light surround the reflection of the grown-up Sarah and the grown-up Sarah faded away into the light, leaving the image of Sarah, the young girl.

Still, she knew the person in the mirror was only who she wished to be.

She remembered the Mirror Man's instruction: "Raise your hands above your head and snap twice, as you did before."

She raised her hands and snapped her fingers—left hand, right hand, both hands—and, again, she could feel a strange, tingling sensation warming her body.

Once again, she was Sarah, the girl.

The Mirror Man smiled when he saw Sarah step from the room of the Seventh Mirror.

"Miss Sarah," he said, bowing. "Now what shall we do?"

"I want to see my mother and father," Sarah told him.

"Indeed," said the Mirror Man. "Then go to them. They're in the mayor's office in the courthouse."

"Come with me," pleaded Sarah.

The Mirror Man knelt before Sarah. He said, "No, Sarah, you need to go alone."

"But I need you," Sarah protested. "To tell them of the magic of the Seventh Mirror." She began to cry quietly.

"No, you only need yourself," the Mirror Man said. "They will never believe the magic of the mirror. But they will believe the magic of having you safely with them." He reached and touched away a tear on Sarah's cheek. "You're the magic, Sarah. You always have been. All children are. All children have magic."

Sarah hugged the Mirror Man.

"Oh, thank you," she said. "I'll never forget you. Never. No matter how old I become."

"And I'll never forget you, Sarah," the Mirror Man told her. "Now, go."

The Mirror Man watched Sarah run across the lawn and disappear into the courthouse. Of all the children he had known, in all the towns and villages, for all the years that he had been the Mirror Man, he had never known anyone as wonderful as Sarah.

He turned back to his wagon-house of mirrors, and he remembered his promise to his father: "Someday, I will look into the mirror. Someday."

He climbed the red fold-down stairs leading into the wagon, and he opened the red door and stepped inside. He stood for a moment, fearful of what he was about to do.

What will I see in the Seventh Mirror? he wondered.

A fisherman?

A lion tamer?

A lawyer?

A mayor?

He smiled. "Not a mayor," he said softly.

He began his funny wobble dance toward the door of the Seventh Mirror.

"Who is that, that Who I see?" he sang in a whisper.

"It is it, or is it me?"

He paused at the door and remembered what he had said to each child as they entered the room of the Seventh Mirror:

"Look into this mirror and you will see,

"Not who you are, but who you wish to be."

Then he said aloud, "It's time to know."

He opened the door and stepped inside and closed his eyes and reached out with his hands until he could feel the Seventh Mirror in front of him. Then he opened his eyes and looked into the mirror.

He blinked in surprise. A smile broke across his face.

For the person he saw in the mirror was himself.

Just as he was.

Fergus Greybar the Fourth.

The Mirror Man.

And, at last, he understood.

Secretly, he had always wished to be the Mirror Man, as his father and his grandfather had been.

His father and his grandfather had brought joy to people.

What could be better than that?